A Note to Parents

Welcome to REAL KIDS READERS, a series of phonics-based books for children who are beginning to read. In the classroom, educators use phonics to teach children how to sound out unfamiliar words, providing a firm foundation for reading skills. At home, you can use REAL KIDS READERS to reinforce and build on that foundation, because the books follow the same basic phonic guidelines that children learn in school.

Of course the best way to help your child become a good reader is to make the experience fun—and REAL KIDS READERS do that, too. With their realistic story lines and lively characters, the books engage children's imaginations. With their clean design and sparkling photographs, they provide picture clues that help new readers decipher the text. The combination is sure to entertain young children and make them truly want to read.

REAL KIDS READERS have been developed at three distinct levels to make it easy for children to read at their own pace.

- LEVEL 1 is for children who are just beginning to read.
- LEVEL 2 is for children who can read with help.
- LEVEL 3 is for children who can read on their own.

A controlled vocabulary provides the framework at each level. Repetition, rhyme, and humor help increase word skills. Because children can understand the words and follow the stories, they quickly develop confidence. They go back to each book again and again, increasing their proficiency and sense of accomplishment, until they're ready to move on to the next level. The result is a rich and rewarding experience that will help them develop a lifelong love of reading.

For Jim and MaryEllen Carlson
—M.L.

Special thanks to Lands' End, Dodgeville, WI, for providing clothing;
to Capezio, New York City, for providing tap shoes; and to
FAO Schwarz, for providing musical instruments.

Copyright © 1998 by Lerner Publishing Group, Inc.

Real Kids Readers and the Real Kids Readers logo
are trademarks of Lerner Publishing Group, Inc.

Produced by DWAI / Seventeenth Street Productions, Inc.
Reading Specialist: Virginia Grant Clammer

Millbrook Press
A division of Lerner Publishing Group, Inc.
241 First Avenue North
Minneapolis, MN 55401 USA

For reading levels and more information, look up this title at www.lernerbooks.com.

Library of Congress Cataloging-in-Publication Data
Leonard, Marcia.
   Big Ben / Marcia Leonard ; photographs by Dorothy Handelman.
      p.   cm. — (Real kids readers. Level 1)
   Summary: Ben becomes a one-man band, honking a horn, ringing bells, singing, clapping,
tapping, and drumming.
      ISBN: 978-0-7613-2013-5 (lib. bdg. : alk. paper)
      ISBN: 978-0-7613-2038-8 (pbk. : alk. paper)
      ISBN: 978-0-7613-7365-0 (eBook)
   [1. Musicians—Fiction. 2. Stories in rhyme.] I. Handleman, Dorothy, ill. II. Title.
III. Series.
PZ8.3.L54925B1 1998
[E]—dc21   98-10041

Manufactured in the United States of America
6-42789-717-8/2/2016

Big Ben

By Marcia Leonard

Photographs by Dorothy Handelman

M Millbrook Press • Minneapolis

Come and see Big Ben.

See Big Ben!

Next Show At
2:00

See his new red cap.

He has two big hands.

He can clap, clap, clap.

He has two fast feet
that can tap the floor.

13

He can make a fist
and tap on the door.

See him honk his horn.

See him play his drum.

He can ring his bells.

He can sing. He can hum.

He can clap, tap, tap
as he sings a song.

He can ring his bells
as he drums along.

When you see Big Ben
you will clap, clap, clap.

29

He is a one-boy band
in a new red cap.

31

Reading with Your Child

1. Try to read with your child at least twenty minutes each day, as part of your regular routine.
2. Keep your child's books in one convenient, cozy reading spot.
3. Read and familiarize yourself with the Phonic Guidelines below.
4. Ask your child to read *Big Ben* out loud. If he or she has difficulty with a word:
    - Help him or her decode the word phonetically. (Say, "Try to sound it out.")
    - Encourage him or her to use picture clues. (Say, "What does the picture show?")
    - Ask him or her to use context clues. (Say, "What would make sense?")
5. If your child still doesn't "get" the word, tell him or her what it is. Don't wait for frustration to build.
6. Praise your beginning reader. With your enthusiasm and encouragement, your child will go from one success to the next.

Phonic Guidelines

Use the following guidelines to help your child read the words in *Big Ben*.

Short Vowels

When two consonants surround a vowel, the sound of the vowel is usually short. This means you pronounce *a* as in apple, *e* as in egg, *i* as in igloo, *o* as in octopus, and *u* as in umbrella. Short-vowel words in this story include: *big, Ben, can, cap, has, him, his, hum, red, tap.*

Short-Vowel Words with Beginning Consonant Blends

When two different consonants begin a word, they usually blend to make a combined sound. Words in this story with beginning consonant blends include: *clap, drum.*

Short-Vowel Words with Ending Consonant Blends

When two different consonants end a word, they usually blend to make a combined sound. Words in this story with ending consonant blends include: *band, fast, fist, hands, honk, ring, sing, song.*

R-Controlled Vowels

When a vowel is followed by the letter *r*, its sound is changed by the *r*. Words in this story with *r*-controlled vowels include: *horn.*

Double Consonants

When two identical consonants appear side by side, one of them is silent. Double-consonant words in this story include: *bells, will.*

Sight Words

Sight words are those words that a reader must learn to recognize immediately—by sight—instead of by sounding them out. They occur with high frequency in easy texts. Sight words not included in the above categories are: *a, and, as, boy, come, he, in, make, new, on, one, play, see, that, the, two, when, you.*